孩子的模仿力強，吸收力佳，在還沒形成地方口音之前，就讓他學習說英語，可避免**晚一天學，多一天困難**的煩惱！外國語言的學習，有助於智力的開發，及見聞的增長。前教育部次長阮大年說：「早學英語的好處很多。我**小學四年級就開始學英語**以致到了台灣唸中學，我一直名列前茅。」

「**學習兒童美語讀本**」1—3冊出版以來，各校老師都認為這套讀本活潑有趣的學習方式，可讓兒童快快樂樂地學會說英語。在各界的鼓勵下，我們配合教育部將英語列入國小選修課程的實施，企劃出齊「**學習兒童美語讀本**」全套六冊，使這套教材更趨完備。

對小朋友而言：本套書以日常生活常遇到的狀況為中心，讓小朋友從身邊的事物開始學英文。實用、生動而有創意的教材，小朋友更能自然親近趣味盎然的英語！

對教學者而言：本套書編序完整，教學者易於整理，各頁教材之下，均有教學提示，老師不必多花時間，就可獲得事半功倍的準備效果。此外，每單元均有唱歌、遊戲、美勞等活動，老師能在輕鬆愉快的方式下，順利教學！

對父母親而言：兒童心理學上，「親子教學法」對孩子學習能力的增強，有很大的幫助。本套書在每單元之後，均附有在家學習的方法，提供具體的方法和技巧，可以幫助家長與子女的共同學習！

透過這套書，兒童學習英語的過程，必然是輕鬆愉快。而且，由於開始時所引發的興趣，未來的學習將充滿興奮與期待！

本 書 特 色

- 學習語言的基本順序，是由 Hearing（聽）、Speaking（説）、Reading（讀）、Writing（寫），本套教材即依此原則編輯。

- **內容背景本土化、國情化**，使兒童在熟悉的環境中學習英語，避免像其他原文兒童英語書，與現實生活有出入的弊端。

- 題材趣味化、生活化，學了立即能在日常生活中使用。

- 將英語歌曲、遊戲，具有創意的美勞，與學習英語巧妙地組合在一起，以提高兒童的學習興趣，達到**寓教於樂**的目的。

- 每單元的教材均有教學指導和提示，**容易教學**。而且每單元之末均列有目標説明，指導者易於掌握重點。

- 提供在家學習的方法，家長們可親自教導自己的子女學習英語，除加強親子關係外，也達到自然的學習成效。

- 每單元終了，附有考查學習成果的習作，有助於指導者了解學生的吸收力。

- 書末附有總複習，以加深學習印象。另外，在下一冊書的前面也有各種方式的複習，以達到溫故知新的目的。

- 本套書以六歲兒童到國二學生為對象，是全國唯一與國中英語課程相銜接的美語教材。學完六冊的小朋友，上了國中，既輕鬆又愉快。

CONTENTS

Review 1 > A. I come on Monday

Look and read.

I come on Monday.

It is my first day.

I fly on Tuesday.

It is my second day.

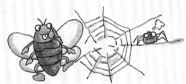
I play on Wednesday.

It is my third day.

I sing on Thursday.

It is my fourth day.

I date on Friday.

It is my fifth day.

I sleep on Saturday.

It is my sixth day.

I go on Sunday.

It is my seventh day.

Oh, it is my last day.

Review 1 ▷ Ⓑ。**When is your birthday?**

Look and say.

① What's the date today ?

② It's May 4th. Tomorrow is Paul's birthday.

③ When is your birthday ?

④ It's March 21.

⑤ What day of the week is it?

⑥ It's Sunday.

⑦ Do you remember when your mother's birthday is ?

⑧ Yes, I do. Her birthday is on April 27th. She likes spring best.

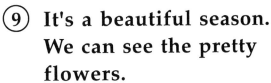

⑨ It's a beautiful season. We can see the pretty flowers.

⑩ I enjoy hiking in the green fields. Which season do you like best ?

⑪ I like summer best. We have long holidays. I can play on the beach and swim in the sea. Do you like winter ?

⑫ No, I don't. It's too cold.

Note : Review "the date" and "seasons of the year". Let students work in pairs and practice the dialogues above until they are familiar with them.

Review 2 ▷ **Who is the fattest?**

Look and say.

A: How many people are there in the picture?
B: There are four people in the picture.
A: Who / Which is the fattest?
B: The blue one is the fattest.
A: Who / Which is the thinnest?
B: The yellow one is the thinnest.
A: Is the blue one taller than the yellow one?
B: No, the blue one is shorter than the yellow one.
A: Do you know who / which is the shortest?
B: The red one is the shortest.

(Note): Review the use of comparatives & superlatives. At first the teacher can ask
questions according to the pictures above. If all the students answer quite well, let
them work in pairs and practice asking and answering each others's questions.

Review 3 > I played tennis yesterday

Look and say.

① Did you play tennis yesterday ?

② Yes, Peter and I played tennis together.

④ No, it was raining when we got there.

⑤ Oh! That's too bad.

③ Was it nice ?

⑦ I was at home and listened to the radio.

⑥ What did you do yesterday ?

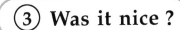

⑨ I know. It's nice and warm outside.

⑧ It's spring now.

⑪ Oh! That's a wonderful idea!

⑩ Let's play tennis tomorrow, OK ?

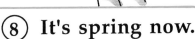

Review 4 ▷ I will study English

Look and say.

study English play volleyball go to the movies clean the floor

A: What will you do after dinner this evening?
B: I will study English.

A: Will you study English tomorrow?
B: Yes, I will. (No, I will not.)

play basketball take a walk swim ski

A: Are you going to play basketball tomorrow?
B: Yes, I am going to play basketball tomorrow.

A: Who is going to be with you?
B: My friend is going to be with me.

 # MARY IS A GOOD GIRL

Mary is a good girl. Many people like her. She always likes to help people. If you ask her for help, she will never say "No". She usually gets up early, so she is never late for school. She usually walks to school, but sometimes she goes to school by bus. In the morning she usually eats a sandwich and drinks milk. She never eats fish in the morning.

She always does her homework in the evening. After dinner she usually cleans her room and washes the dishes.

On Sunday she always goes to church. She is often busy on Sunday, but she never forgets to help her mother.

Everyone is always glad to see her. Have you ever seen her?

1 ALWAYS, USUALLY & OFTEN

1. In the morning I

| always
usually
often
sometimes
never | eat | bread.
sandwiches.
hamburgers.
fish.
fruit. |

2. On Sunday we

| always
usually
often
sometimes
never | go | to the beach.
to church.
to the movies.
to the market. |

3. We are

| always
usually
often
sometimes
never | busy on Saturday. |

4. In the evening I

| always
usually
often
sometimes
never | do my homework. |

5. Does John

| always
usually
often
sometimes
ever | clean his room? |

 **LET'S PRACTICE**

Look and say.

A : Do you ever <u>watch TV</u> <u>on Monday</u>?

B : No, I don't.

A : When do you watch TV?

B : I <u>always watch TV on Sunday</u>.

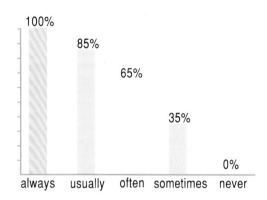

100% 85% 65%

watch TV

100% 65% 35%

take a bus

85% 65% 0%

clean the living room

100% 35% 0%

go to English class

85% 35% 0%

drink milk

65% 35% 0%

brush my teeth

(Note) : Let students work in pairs. Take turns asking and answering questions with "always", "often", "usually", etc.

LEARN A RHYME

Do and say.

Listen To Me

Mark is always watching TV.
He never listens to me!
Mary is usually listening to the radio.
She never listens to me!
Susan and Jack are always reading.
They never listen to me!
The cat is often sleeping on the floor.
It never listens to me!
I am right. I am always right.
But nobody wants to listen to me!

EXERCISE

Rearrange the sentences.

Example:　usually the morning Do you get up in late?

Do you usually get up late in the morning?

1. you Do watch television the evening in always?

   _____

2. to school never I go late.

   _____

3. usually by train She goes to work.

   _____

4. often busy Are on Sunday you?

   _____

5. to school John and Mary always walk.

   _____

6. in the park Jack plays usually.

   _____

■ **本單元目標**：讓學生學習各種頻率副詞用法及位置，此種複雜的排列更能激發孩子們的組合能力。

■ **在家學習的方法**：媽媽可將句子用口頭念出，一面訓練小孩聽力，一面教他們組合正確的句子。

2 QUANTITY (I)

1 some

1. Susan has **some** toys.
2. Peter has **some** stamps.
3. Mark bought **some** pencils for his brother.
4. Mother cooked **some** potatoes for Mary.

2 any

A: Are there **any** story books on the desk?
B: No, there are **no** story books on the desk.
A: Did he buy **any** toys for his children?
B: Yes, he bought **some** toys for his children.

③ a few

1. He found **a few** pencils in the pencilbox.
2. Jack only has **a few** friends.
3. There are **a few** pictures on the wall.
4. My father planted **a few** trees in our garden.

④ a little

1. There is only **a little** water in the kettle.
2. There is only **a little** milk in the cup.
3. Could you please give me **a little** jam?
4. Bill only has **a little** money.

(Note) : few = not many
little = not much

 **LET'S PRACTICE**

Read and match.

There are some broken chairs in the classroom.

There is only a little food in the refrigerator.

I'm sorry! I don't have any money to pay you.

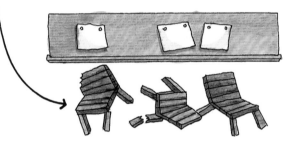

There isn't any milk in the bottle.

They found a few toys under the bed.

PLAY A GAME

What am I doing?

(Note) : This is a guessing game. The teacher divides the class into two groups. Each student must think of a thing to do and act it out in front of his group. They must make the other team members guess what they are doing faster than the other team. Two students, one from each group, will go to the board. The teacher will give each student an idea. For example, *riding a bicycle, driving a car, closing a window*, etc. The students will try to make the other students guess. When one group gets the right answer, the student at the front sits down and another student in the group gets up and goes to the front. That team will get one point. The teacher will then give that student a new idea. The team with the most points after 10 to 15 minutes wins.

■**本單元目標**：學習some、any、a little、a few的用法及可數名詞、不可數名詞的觀念。

■**在家學習的方法**：家長可以利用課文的圖片向孩子們說明可數名詞及不可數名詞的區別，再教他們 some、any、a little、a few 的用法。平常在家中，也可把握機會，讓孩子們用這些字詞造句。

EXERCISE

Answer questions.

1. Does Susan have any toys ?

   _____

2. How many toys do you have ?

   _____

3. Who has some stamps ?

   _____

4. How many pencils does Mark buy ?

   _____

5. How many friends does Jack have ?

   _____

6. How many pictures are there on the wall ?

   _____

7. Is there much milk in the cup ?

   _____

8. Have you got any stamps ?

   _____

(Note) : Ask students the above questions. If your class is doing well so far, you may let students take over your role as questioner.

3 QUANTITY (II)

5 a lot of

1. There are **a lot of** animals in the forest.
2. I need **a lot of** friends.
3. Do you need **a lot of** money?
4. There is **a lot of** food on the table.

6 many

1. How **many** trees are there in the garden?
2. There are **many** people in the park.
3. That lady has **many** pairs of shoes.
4. There are not **many** pencilboxes on the desk.

7 much

1. He hasn't got **much** hair.
2. There isn't **much** milk in the bottle.
3. She doesn't eat **much** food.
4. How **much** money do you have?

Grammar Point

- much
  a little } + uncountable nouns
- many
  a few } + countable nouns
- a lot of
  some
  any } + countable or uncountable nouns

■本單元目標：延續上一課的課程，介紹a lot of、many、much的用法。
■在家學習的方法：可讓孩子們先從"much milk"、"many trees"等詞組開始練習，再教他們造完整的句子。

3-1 LET'S PRACTICE

Choose the correct one.

1. I am very hungry. I didn't eat_____ breakfast this morning.
(a) much   (b) many
(c) any   (d) little

2. There are _____ books in the library.
(a) much   (b) a little
(c) any   (d) a lot of

3. How_____ pencils do you have ?
(a) some   (b) many
(c) a little   (d) any

4. Do you have _____ envelopes ?
(a) any   (b) little
(c) a little   (d) much

5. How_____ does the skirt cost ?
(a) many   (b) a few
(c) much   (d) a little

6. He will stay in my house for_____ days.
(a) a few   (b) much
(c) any   (d) a little

7. My sister needs_____ eggs for the cakes.
(a) much   (b) a little
(c) some   (d) any

8. Don't drink too_____ coffee.
(a) many   (b) little
(c) a few   (d) much

SING A SONG

If You're Happy

1. if you're hap-py and you know it, clap your hands. (clap, clap)

If you're hap-py and you know it, clap your hands. (clap, clap)

If you're hap-py and you know it, then your face will sure-ly show it.

If you're hap-py and you know it, clap your hands. (clap, clap)

1. clap your hands
2. tap your head
3. nod your head
4. touch your toes

5. turn around
6. bend your knees
7. stamp your feet
8. laugh out loud

EXERCISE

Make sentences.

1. some

_____

2. any (negative)

_____

3. any (question)

_____

4. a few

_____

5. a little

_____

6. a lot of

_____

7. many

_____

8. much

_____

(Note) : Review "some", "any", "a few", "a little", "a lot of", "many" and "much". Have students learn each word and learn how to make sentences until everyone can read and write. Don't forget to tell them the difference between countable and uncountable nouns.

4 THIS IS YOUR DOG, ISN'T IT?

Mary : This is your dog, isn't it?
Tom : Yes, it is. His name is Baby.

Mary : He's cute.
Tom : Do you like dogs?

Mary : Yes, I like dogs very much. But my mother doesn't like dogs, so I can't have a dog.
Tom : Well, that's too bad.

Mary : Does Baby sleep in your house at night?
Tom : No, he doesn't. He sleeps in the doghouse.

Mary : Do you take him for a walk every day?
Tom : Yes, I must take him to the park every day.

Mary : Do you take him to the park in the morning?
Tom : No, I get up late, and I'm always busy in the morning.

Mary : When do you take him for a walk?
Tom : I take him for a walk sometimes before dinner and sometimes after dinner.

Mary : Baby likes the park, doesn't he?
Tom : Yes, he is always happy in the park.

Mary : Do you always walk with Baby in the park?

(Note) : **Divide the class into two teams. One is to be Tom; the other Mary. If they can read all their parts, then change roles. The teacher can also choose two students to do the reading.**

Tom : No, I usually throw my tennis ball and he brings it back to me in his mouth.

Mary : Oh, does he ? He's very smart, isn't he ?

Tom : Yes, he is. I come home every day at three, and he is always waiting for me at the gate.

Mary : He is so white, too. You wash him, don't you ?

Tom : Yes, I wash him every Sunday afternoon.

Mary : It's difficult, isn't it ?

Tom : No, it's easy. He enjoys it, too.

Mary : You wash him in the bathroom, don't you ?

Tom : In winter I wash him in the bathroom, but in summer I wash him in the yard.

4-1 LET'S PRACTICE

Answer questions.

1. What's the dog's name ?
2. Does Mary's mother like dogs ?
3. Does Tom take his dog to the park in the morning ?
4. When does Tom take Baby for a walk ?
5. Baby likes the park, doesn't he ?
6. Baby is very smart, isn't he ?
7. Where does Tom wash his dog ?
8. Do you like dogs ?
9. Do you have any pets ?

■ 本單元目標：學習附加問句的用法。

1. Be動詞	2. 普通動詞	3. 助動詞
is⇄isn't	do⇄don't	can⇄can't
are⇄aren't	does⇄doesn't	could⇄couldn't
was⇄wasn't	did⇄didn't	will⇄won't
were⇄weren't		would⇄wouldn't
		should⇄shouldn't

■ 在家學習的方法：家長可先讓孩子們練習造肯定的附加問句，再加入否定的附加問句。

4-2 PLAY A GAME

Get the apple.

1. She bought some oranges.
2. She didn't buy any oranges.

(x) ⇨

1. You like fish.
2. You don't like fish.

(o)

(o)

1. Mark doesn't like eating.
2. Mark likes to eat.

(x) ⇨

1. I am not tired.
2. I am tired.

(o)

(o)

1. We should do it.
2. We shouldn't do it.

(x) ⇨

1. They couldn't do it.
2. They could do it.

(o)

(o)

1. Mary was at home last night.
2. Mary wasn't at home last night.

(x) ⇨

1. It didn't rain yesterday.
2. It rained yesterday.

(o)

(o)

1. You will go to the party.
2. You won't go to the party.

(x) ⇨ **You must study hard!**

(Note) : Let each students make tag-questions. If the player answers correctly, he then proceeds to the next question below (marked "O"). Otherwise he follows the path marked "X".

EXERCISE

Make tag-questions.

Example:

> **Baby is a good dog.**
>
> **Baby is a good dog, isn't he?**

(1)   You also like dogs.

_____

(2)   He would wash it in the bathroom.

_____

(3)   Mark will play baseball tomorrow.

_____

(4)   Susan and Paul are good friends.

_____

(5)   She didn't go to school yesterday.

_____

(6)   He doesn't like to dance.

_____

(7)   We should do it.

_____

(8)   Helen wasn't happy last night.

_____

PASSIVE VOICE

English is a very important language today. It's spoken in the United States. In Taiwan and many other countries it's taught at school as a foreign language.

English is very useful when people from different countries need to talk with each other.

5 VERB FORMS

A

use	used	used
clean	cleaned	cleaned
wash	washed	washed
call	called	called
move	moved	moved
like	liked	liked
play	played	played
carry	carried	carried
study	studied	studied

B

buy	bought	bought
get	got	gotten
eat	ate	eaten
write	wrote	written
teach	taught	taught
give	gave	given
make	made	made
say	said	said
run	ran	run
see	saw	seen
do	did	done
know	knew	known
speak	spoke	spoken
take	took	taken
drink	drank	drunk

5-1 LET'S PRACTICE

Read and do.

 Read the story. Then number the pictures in the correct order.

An ant was drinking water from a stream. Suddenly, it fell into the stream and was carried away. A bird saw the ant and tried to save it by dropping a leaf into the stream. The ant was able to reach land safely.

Shortly after, the ant saw a hunter trying to shoot the bird. The ant quickly ran up the hunter's leg and bit him. The hunter moved, so he missed the bird. The bird flew away.

The ant was very happy that it was able to help the bird.

SING A SONG

Looby Loo

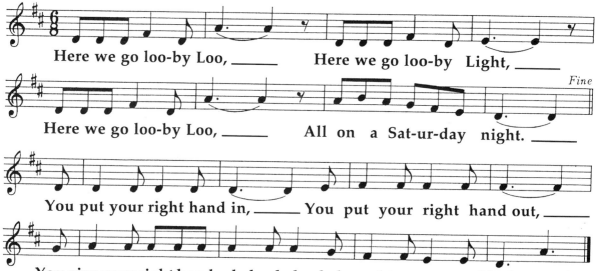

Here we go loo-by Loo, _____ Here we go loo-by Light, _____

Here we go loo-by Loo, _____ All on a Sat-ur-day night. _____

You put your right hand in, _____ You put your right hand out, _____

You give your right hand a shake, shake, shake, and turn your-self a-bout. Oh,

You put your left hand in,
You put your left hand out,
You give your left hand a
Shake, shake, shake,

You put your left foot in,
You put your left foot out,
You give your left foot a
Shake, shake, shake,

You put your whole self in,
You put your whole self out,
You give your whole self a
Shake, shake, shake,

You put your right foot in,
You put your right foot out,
You give your right foot a
Shake, shake, shake,

You put your right hand out,
You put your right hand in,
You give your right hand a
Shake, shake, shake,

EXERCISE

Rearrange the sentences.

1. Example: John, was, ball, that, picked, by up.

➡ **That ball was picked up by John.**

1. him, English, are, taught, by, we.

    _____

2. was, I, made, happy, them, by.

    _____

3. Canada, English, spoken, is, in.

    _____

4. liked, everybody, he, is, by.

    _____

5. every day, cleaned, the classroom, is.

    _____

6. Mark, yesterday, washed, was, the car, by.

    _____

7. rice, eaten, is, Taiwan, in.

    _____

8. house, is, painted, his.

    _____

2. **Example:** Helen washed the dishes.

➡ **The dishes were washed by Helen.**

1. Mary cleans her room.

   _____

2. He teaches us English.

   _____

3. A car ran over the dog.

   _____

4. Mark wrote the letter.

   _____

5. He closes his store at six.

   _____

6. Our teachers use this room.

   _____

■本單元目標：學習被動態的使用：be動詞＋p.p.

■在家學習的方法：首先可先教孩子們背誦動詞三態的方法，讓他們像歌唱一樣地記住這些動詞變化。然後家長可試著唸主動態的句子，讓孩子們改成被動態，一直到他們熟練為止。

6 ♠ RELATIVE PRONOUNS

1.

A: Look at the girl who is waiting for the bus. Do you know her?

B: Yes, she is Mary's sister, Helen.

A: Mary? You mean that pretty girl?

B: That's right! Everyone knows that pretty girl. We are green with envy.

A: Green with envy?

B: Yes, we use the word "green" when we envy someone. Look it up in your dictionary.

2.

A: What's the matter with you?

B: I can't do the math homework which was given to us yesterday.

A: Don't worry. I'll help you.

B: Oh, Jack! Thank you so much.

A: You are welcome. A friend in need is a friend indeed.

6 ♠ **WHO, WHICH & THAT**

1

{ **The boy** is my brother.
{ **The boy** plays tennis.

The boy who plays tennis is my brother.

2

{ **The book** is on the desk.
{ I bought **the book** yesterday.

The book which I bought yesterday is on the desk.

3

{ **The old man and his dog** live next to us.
{ **The old man and his dog** are crossing the street.

The old man and his dog that are crossing the street live next to us.

4

{ **The cookies** are good.
{ **They** were made by Mary.

The cookies which were made by Mary are good.

5

{ Here is **a record**.
{ My father gave me **the record** yesterday.

Here is the record which my father gave me yesterday.

6-1 LET'S PRACTICE

Look and say.

Look at the boy. He is swimming in the pool.

Look at the boy who is swimming in the pool.

I know the girl.
She is playing the guitar.

I can see a dog.
It is running along the street.

I like the story.
It was written by Mark Twain.

This is a car.
It was made in Taiwan.

Jack is my friend.
He lives in Canada.

The cat is "Kitty."
It is sleeping under the table.

(Note) : Tell the students not to write answers in their books. Let volunteers read the
answers aloud and write them on the blackboard.

PLAY A GAME

Make a guess.

Hint:

1. a. Jane is a girl *who* has long hair.
    b. Jane is a girl *who* wears glasses.
    c. Jane is a girl *whose* hair is black.

2. a. Betty is a girl *who* has a letter.
    b. Betty has a letter *which* Tom wrote to her.
    c. Betty has a letter *which* has three stamps on the envelope.

Answer: Jane = (   )

Betty = (   )

EXERCISE

Make sentences.

1. Susan has a pen pal. She lives in Canada.

   ⇨ **Susan has a pen pal who lives in Canada.**
   _____

2. I know a boy. He can draw pictures very well.

   ⇨
   _____

3. We will visit a girl. She was sick yesterday.

   ⇨
   _____

4. The girl was very kind. She talked to me.

   ⇨
   _____

5. I saw a baby lion. It was playing with its mother.

   ⇨
   _____

6. She had a dog. She loved it very much.

   ⇨
   _____

7. I have an old camera. It was given to me by my father.

   ⇨
   _____

■本單元目標：學習如何使用關係代名詞"that"、"who"、及"which"。本課中的習題務必親自動手寫，才能眞正了解。

■在家學習的方法：家長可先唸出２個相關句子，再讓孩子們用關係代名詞連接起來；等他們熟練之後，再讓他們看著圖，造完整的句子。

7 I ENJOY COOKING

"Let's talk about ourselves," says Miss Wang. "Mark likes to write letters. I like to go mountain climbing. What do you like, Susan?"

"I like to collect stamps. It is interesting to collect stamps," says Susan. "What do you like to do, Helen?"

"I enjoy cooking very much. I try to help my mother. On Sunday I go to the store. I buy food and cook it."

John stands up. "I like to study English. I want to understand other countries."

"Good," says Miss Wang. "You also like using the library. Is that right?"

"Yes, it is."

"Studying English is important. No matter where you go, you need English," says Miss Wang. "What do you like to do, Wayne?"

"I love to play baseball. Playing baseball is fun."

"Good," says Miss Wang. "Playing baseball is good exercise. Exercise is good for your health."

7-1 LET'S PRACTICE

Look and read.

(1)

| Swimming
Playing baseball
Collecting stamps
Climbing mountains | is | my favorite activity.
a good hobby. |

(2)

It is | important
interesting
easy
good for us | to study English.

= Studying English is | important.
interesting.
easy.
good for us.

(3)

I | like
love
hate | to read it.

(4)

I | like
love
hate
enjoy | reading it.

(5) Compare:

| **A** | I forgot to mail this letter.
I forgot mailing this letter. |

| **B** | I stopped to study English.
I stopped studying English. |

Note： Let students know the differences between (A) "forgot + to + V." and "forgot + Ving",(B) "stopped + Ving" and "stopped + to + V."

7-2 PLAY A GAME

You scream, I scream, we all scream for ice cream.

She sells sea-shells by the sea shore.

Mabel, Mabel, young and able, take your elbows off the table.

Peter Piper picked a peck of pickled peppers.

Betty Botter bought some butter.

Roses are red. Violets are blue. Sugar is sweet. And so are you.

EXERCISE

Look and write.

I enjoy playing tennis very much.
Playing tennis is my favorite activity.

Look and say.

| look at stars | dance | play tennis | learn English |

Example: Looking at stars is very interesting.

Look and write.

1. Susan starts to write a letter.
   Susan starts writing a letter.

2. It began to rain.

3. My brother likes to watch TV.

4. They hate to go to school on Sunday.

■**本單元目標**：學習動名詞當主詞，及某些特定動詞如"enjoy"、"like"等動名詞的用法。請注意"stop"和"forget"這兩個動詞後面接動名詞(Ving)和不定詞(to V.)時各表不同的意思。

■**在家學習的方法**：家長可利用本課的表格，向孩子們講解動名詞的各種句型，並讓他們自己造句，加深記憶。

8 IT TASTES GOOD

Susan **looks** beautiful.
She **looks like** her mother.

This cake **tastes** good.
It **tastes like** a chocolate cake.

The dish which was cooked by Helen **smells** delicious.
It **smells like** fish.

Mark **feels** tired.

It **feels like** a cat.

The story **sounds** boring.

Wayne feels confused **and** John feels confused, too.

Peter seems satisfied, **but** Tom seems hungry.

Both Jack **and** Bill study English hard.

Mother **not only** cooked dinner **but also** washed the dishes.

Bill **not only** ate a large hamburger **but also** drank a large glass of coke.

■本單元目標：學習連綴動詞"look"、"seem"、"taste"、"smell"、"sound"、"feel"的用法，
及not only～but also～的句型。

■在家學習的方法：家長可先給予孩子們「連綴動詞＋形容詞」及「連綴動詞＋like＋名
詞」的觀念，再讓他們看著課本上的圖片，練習造句。

LET'S PRACTICE

Look and say.

⇨ **Mary not only finished the homework but also helped her mother.**

fat / ugly

read the book / saw the movie

wrote a letter / cleaned her room

smells good / tastes good

(Use these words: taste, look, sound, feel)

⇨ **Father feels comfortable.**

delicious

nice

sour

interesting

SING A SONG

Edelweiss

E - del - weiss,   E - del - weiss,

Ev - 'ry   morn-ing you   greet   me.

Small   and   white,   Clean   and   bright,

You   look   hap-py   to   meet   me.

Blos - som of   snow, may you bloom and   grow,

Bloom and   grow   for - ev   -   er.

E - del - weiss,   E - del - weiss,

Bless   my   home-land for - ev   -   er.

8-3 EXERCISE

Answer questions.

Example: How does Mary's dress look? **(nice)**
➡ **It looks very nice.**

(1) How does this picture look? **(bad)**

_____

(2) How do you feel after school? **(tired)**

_____

(3) What does the earth look like? **(a ball)**

_____

(4) How does the cookie taste? **(delicious)**

_____

(5) How does the music sound? **(sweet)**

_____

(6) What does the food taste like? **(beef)**

_____

(7) How did the story sound? **(exciting)**

_____

(8) How does the air smell? **(fresh)**

_____

9 SOUR GRAPES

Once there was a fox who was very, very hungry. "I am **so** hungry **that** I could eat a horse," he thought.

He looked and looked, but still he could find nothing to eat. At last he came to a high stone wall. The fox stood at the bottom and looked up.

There, at the top of the wall, were the most beautiful grapes he had ever seen. They were **so** beautiful **that** they made his mouth water.

The fox stood on his back legs, but could not reach them. He jumped as high as he could, but it was no use. The wall was too high for him.

The fox turned away sadly. "I don't want those grapes anyway," he said. "They're **so** green **that** they're probably sour."

 **LET'S PRACTICE**

Look and say.

A

You're very late.
You can't take the bus.
➡ **You are too late to take the bus.**

B

John is very busy.
He can't go to the party.
➡ **John is so busy that he can't go to the party.**

① The question is very difficult.
We can not answer it.

① She was very scared.
She could not move.

② My father is very busy.
He can't watch TV.

② It is very cold.
I can't go out.

③ The man was very old.
He couldn't drive a car.

③ I was very sick.
I could not go to school.

SING A SONG

SING

9-3 EXERCISE

Change the sentences with "so ~ that".

Example: Your brother is too young to go to school.

➡ **Your brother is so young that he can't go to school.**

1. Jack was too thirsty to study.

   _____

2. The tea is too hot for me to drink.

   _____

3. I was too shy to speak in public.

   _____

4. The driver was too busy to come.

   _____

5. I was too late to watch the cartoon.

   _____

6. The question is too difficult for him to answer.

   _____

7. He is too old to dance.

   _____

Join the two sentences with "so ~ that" or "too ~ to".

Example: I was late. She got angry. **(so ~ that)**
➡ **I was so late that she got angry.**

The driver was busy. He couldn't come. **(too ~ to)**
➡ **The driver was too busy to come.**

1. It's noisy near an airport. You can't sleep well. **(so ~ that)**

_____

2. Your brother is young. He can't go to school. **(too ~ to)**

_____

3. The question is difficult for him. He can't answer it.
    (too ~ to)

_____

4. He spoke fast. I could not understand him. **(so ~ that)**

_____

5. I was late. I couldn't catch the bus. **(too ~ to)**

_____

6. The book was interesting. I read it many times. **(so ~ that)**

_____

7. The tea is hot. I can't drink it. **(too ~ to)**

_____

■本單元目標：學習用"so～that"及"too～to"的句型來造句。
■在家學習的方法：家長可先讓孩子們看圖造句，等熟練之後，再做習題。課文部分可用互相講故事的方式來增加孩子們的學習興趣。

10 HOW TERRIBLE!

John : Hi, Mom! Will you wash this for me?

Mom: **What a dirty shirt!** Wait a minute.

John : Oh, I'm sorry. I forgot. It's my report card.

Mom: **What bad grades! How terrible!** What will Dad say?

JOhn	REPORT	CARD	
PERIOD	COURSE	TEACHER	1 st
1	MATHEMATICS	SMITH	D
2	NATURAL SCIENCE	JONES	C⁻
3	P.E	DAVIS	B
4	CHINESE	CHEN	D⁺
5	SOCIAL SCIENCE	FOSTER	C
6	HISTORY	TURNER	A

John : Dad, I got a D in math.

Dad : Now listen. Grades are important but they are not everything. Take it easy, John.

Mom : But he must work harder. He is practicing basketball too much these days.

John : How were your high school grades, Dad?

Dad : Well, I once got a D in math, too. Even some famous men like Edison got bad grades.

Mom : **What a good excuse!**

10 MAKE, WATCH & HEAR

1 Mary helped Mother cook breakfast.

2 Mother didn't let us play baseball yesterday.

3 Susan watched us play in the park.

4 Sad movies make me cry.

5 We felt the classroom move.

6 John heard Mary sing a song.

10-1 LET'S PRACTICE

Look and say.

A ▷

It is a very tall tree.
➡ **What a tall tree it is!**

① She has very beautiful flowers.

② It was a nice party.

○	成	績	單 ○
	科 目		分 數
1	自 然		38
2	國 語		49
3	數 學		50

③ They are bad grades.

B ▷

John is very hungry.
➡ **How hungry John is.**

① The book is very interesting.

② Paul is very tall.

③ Nancy was sad.

■**本單元目標**：學習如何將直述句改為「感嘆句」。並練習用「感官動詞」如 "watch"、"hear"、"see"、"feel" 等，和「使役動詞」如 "let"、"make" 等來造句。

■**在家學習的方法**：家長可多利用身邊的事物讓孩子們造感嘆句。另外課文中的對話部分，可採取角色扮演的方式學習。

PLAY A GAME

Make a paper crane.

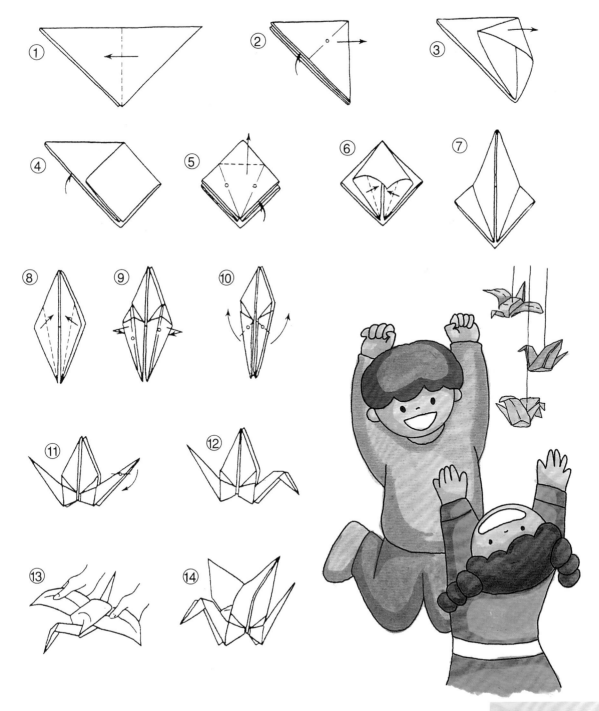

10-3 EXERCISE

Make sentences.

A ▷

1. How busy he is.   busy

2. _____ old

3. _____ glad

4. _____ pretty

5. What a big apple.   big

6. _____ kind

7. _____ small

8. _____ beautiful

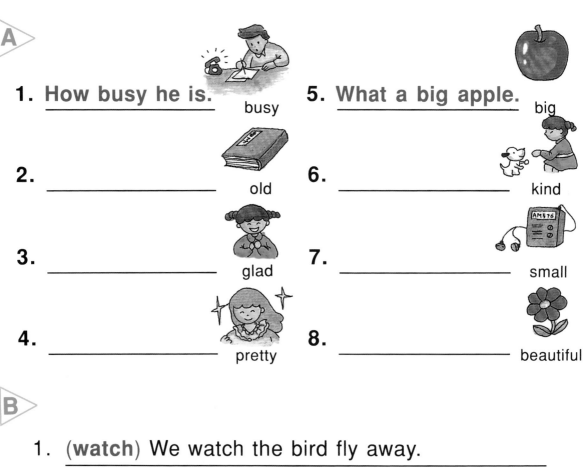

B ▷

1. (**watch**) We watch the bird fly away.

2. (**make**) _____

3. (**hear**) _____

4. (**let**) _____

5. (**see**) _____

6. (**feel**) _____

7. (**help**) _____

11 EITHER & NEITHER

We can speak **either** English **or** Chinese in the classroom.

I will **neither** watch TV **nor** study English.

Helen will eat **neither** a hamburger **nor** a hot dog.

I will **either** ride a bicycle **or** take a bus to school.

Either you **or** Tom is correct.

Neither Mary **nor** Helen has to sweep the floor.

(Note) : "Neither ~ nor" is the negative form of "either ~ or". You say "either ~ or" when you can do one or the other, but not both. But when you can't even do one, you use "neither ~ nor".

11 SO DO I

1. John has a new car, and I do, too.
   = John has a new car.
     So do I.

2. Mary cooked breakfast, and I did, too.
   = Mary cooked breakfast.
     So did I.

3. John doesn't have a new car, and I don't, either.
   = John doesn't have a new car.
     Neither do I.
     Nor do I.

4. Mary didn't cook breakfast, and I didn't, either.
   = Mary didn't cook breakfast.
     Neither did I.
     Nor did I.

 # 11-1 LET'S PRACTICE

Look and say.

basketball soccer
play

You can play either basketball or soccer.

eat at a
restaurant   cook at home

sweater shirt
buy

hamburger noodles
eat

ride a bicycle take a taxi

magazine dictionary
choose

Mark doesn't like monkeys.
He doesn't like snakes, either.

⇨ **Mark likes neither monkeys nor snakes.**

Nancy doesn't want a skirt.
She doesn't want a sweater,
either.

Helen didn't drink coffee.
She didn't eat any
hamburgers, either.

Bill can't sing very well.
He can't ride a bicycle very well, either.

John wouldn't like to order a
coke.
He wouldn't like to order a
milkshake, either.

Tom is not tall.
He is not fat, either.

11-2 SING A SONG

Do-Re-Mi

11-3 EXERCISE

Look and write.

 A

1. John likes my friend. **So do I.**
   I do, too.

2. Mary's tired today. _____
   _____

3. John doesn't have a sweater. _____
   _____

4. Nancy is not a teacher. _____
   _____

5. Mark didn't bring his umbrella. _____
   _____

 B

1. You, can, buy

   You can buy either a baseball or a
   basketball.

2. Bill, drink

_____

3. Peter, Wayne, will go fishing

_____

4. My father, order

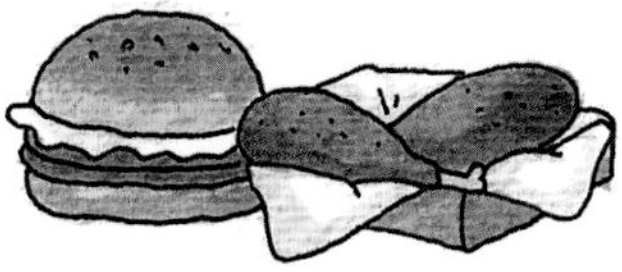

_____

5. Susan, Nancy, sweep

_____

6. Wayne, want

_____

7. Peter

_____

8. Helen, can

_____

■本單元目標：練習"neither～nor～"及"either～or～"的句型。注意"neither～nor～"及"either～or～"兩邊所接的詞性必需一致。
在家學習的方法：家長可利用圖表先敎孩子們如何將"I do, too"及"I don't, either"改成倒裝句。再告訴他們"either～or～"為「兩者其中之一」，"neither～nor～"則為「兩者皆不是」的差別。

12 I HAVE READ IT

(1)

| I We You They | have | studied English lived in Taipei read this book | for a long time. for two years. |

(2)

| Helen John | has | visited Singapore used the dictionary | many times. |

(3) Susan has

| already just | finished her homework.

(4) Have

| you they | ever

| seen that movie? read that novel? |

Has

| he John | finished his breakfast

| already? yet? |

(5) Yes,

| I they | have.   No,

| I they | haven't.

Yes,

| she he | has.   No,

| she he | hasn't.

(Note) : Teach students how to use the words like "for a long time", "since last year", "ever", "yet" and "already".

 A TRIP TO THE USA

John's family studied the map of the United States. They have made plans to see many different places during the summer vacation. They have made reservations in Philadelphia and Boston.

They have visited Florida so they made plans to go to Texas, Arizona, and California. Then they will visit Chicago and Detroit. Niagara Falls has been in their plans since they decided to go to the United States. From there they will stop in Canada and fly to London.

John wants to go to Texas to see real cowboys. Mary wants to see the Grand Canyon in Arizona. Everybody wants to see Disneyland in California. It is very famous.

⭐ Oral quiz.

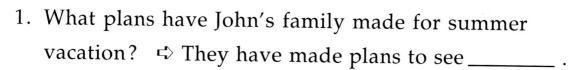

1. What plans have John's family made for summer
   vacation? ⇨ They have made plans to see _____ .

2. Where do they plan to go?
   ⇨ They plan to go _____ .

3. What does John want to see in
   Texas? ⇨ He wants_____ .

4. What does Mary want to see in
   Arizona? ⇨ She wants _____ .

5. Have you ever seen real cowboys?

6. Has your father visited the United
   States?

7. Have you ever been to Florida before?

 **LET'S PRACTICE**

Look and say.

Example: A: How long have you <u>lived in Taipei</u>?
　　　　　　　B: <u>I've lived here for ten years.</u>

**study English
for two years**

**be sick
for a long time**

**stay in the U.S.A.
for three years**

A: 　 Have you decided what to do this winter?
You: Yes, I plan to _____
A: 　 That's great. I've never _____ before.
You: What are you going to do this winter?
A: 　 I want to _____ but _____

(Note) : Let students work in pairs and use the dialogue model to talk about their plans for
　　　　this winter.

PLAY A GAME

Who did what?

> I've visited Tainan, and he has visited New York, and...

Note : The teacher writes these verbs on the board: *been, seen, visited, decided, made, read, eaten*, etc. The students, one at a time, will make up and say a sentence using one of these verbs. The next student will say his/her sentence and add what the other students said about himself/herself.

The first students to pause too long or make a mistake must drop out of the game. The next student starts a new game with another verb.

12-3 EXERCISE

Make sentences.

① **I live in this city.** (for ten years)

   I have lived in this city for ten years.

② **They live in Taiwan.** (for a long time)

   _____

③ **My brother washes the car.** (for two hours)

   _____

④ **He is sick.** (for a long time)

   _____

⑤ **I opened all the windows.** (just)

   _____

⑥ **I finish my homework.** (already)

   _____

⑦ **My mother and father didn't come home.** (yet)

   _____ _____

⑧ **He visits Europe.** (several times)

   _____

⑨ **Did you see that movie?** (ever)

   _____

■本單元目標：學習現在完成式的句型。

■在家學習的方法：家長可先幫孩子們複習動詞的三態變化，再教他們現在完成式的
　公式"have(has)＋P.P."，進而練習造肯定句、否定句到疑問句。

13 WHAT WOULD YOU DO?

One day Mark and Jack were walking through a park. They were on their way to the library.

They took a rest under an old tree in the park.

Jack found that there was a wallet with a lot of money in it. He said, "Someone must have lost it. I should take it to the police station." Mark answered, "If I were you, I would wait here, because he might come back to look for his wallet."

What would you do?

 **13-1 LET'S PRACTICE**

Look and say.

(A) Example:

I don't have any money so I can't buy a new car.
⇨ **If** I **had** some money, I **could buy** a new car.

I don't have time so I won't do my homework.

We don't have a holiday so we can't go camping.

I'm not rich so I can't travel around the world.

Jack doesn't take off his coat so he won't catch a cold.

I don't have a dictionary so I can't look up the word.

I am not a bird so I can't fly.

(B) Example:

John has time.
He writes a letter to me. ⇨ **If John has time, he will write a letter to me.**

Peter finishes his work.
He goes to the party.

The movie is popular.
They go to see the movie.

Susan is sick. She stays home and rests.

Jack studies hard.
He gets good grades.

The weather is fine.
They go on a picnic.

They go to the beach.
They wear swimming suits.

(Note) : Teach students the difference between the two patterns above. One is the opposite of the present situation; the other may happen in the future.

13-2 SING A SONG

Donna Donna

♩= 96

Dm   A7   Dm   A7   Dm   Gm

On a wag - on   bound for mar - ket   There's a calf with a

Dm   A7   Dm   A7   Dm   A7

mourn-ful eye.   High a-bove – him   there's a swal - low

Dm   Gm   Dm   A7 Dm   C   C7

Wing-ing swift - ly – through the sky.   How the winds are

F   C   C7   F   Dm

laugh- ing.   They laugh with all   their might.

C   C7   F   Dm   A7

Laugh and laugh the whole day through and half the sum-mer's

Dm   A7   Dm

night.   Don-na, Don-na, Don - na, Don - na. –

C   C7   F   A7

Don-na, Don-na, Don - na, – Don.   Don-na, Don-na, Don - na,

Dm   A7   Dm

Don - na. –   Don-na, Don-na, Don - na, Don.

13-3 EXERCISE

Make sentences.

(A) Example: the weather/fine/we/go picnicking

➡ **If the weather is fine, we will go picnicking.**

1. I/have time/write to you.

   _____

2. my brother/has a car/drive to school.

   _____

3. we/have a holiday/go camping in the mountains.

   _____

4. he/has some money/buy a new bicycle.

   _____

5. you/are rich/go around the world.

   _____

6. she/knows/tell about it.

   _____

7. you/take off your coat/catch a cold.

   _____

8. I/go to the party/tell you.

   _____

(B) Example: If the weather is fine, we will go picnicking.
➡ **If the weather was fine, we would go picnicking.**

(Change the sentences on page 76.)

1.

2.

3.

4.

5.

6.

7.

8.

■**本單元目標**：學習If的假設句及條件句，注意兩者之間的差別。
　①「If＋過去式，～Would/could/might/should＋原形動詞」表與現在事實相反的
　　假設。　②「If＋現在式，～will＋原形動詞」表未來可能實現的條件句。
■**在家學習的方法**：家長可先告訴孩子們「與現在事實相反的假設句」和「有可能實現
　的條件句」之間的區別，再讓他們親自動手寫習題，等他們熟悉之後，再給予圖說的練
　習。

Review 1 ▷ The Irregular Verbs

	simple present	simple past	past participle
①	be (am, is / are)	was / were	been
②	become	became	become
③	begin	began	begun
④	break	broke	broken
⑤	bring	brought	brought
⑥	build	built	built
⑦	buy	bought	bought
⑧	can	could	—
⑨	catch	caught	caught
⑩	come	came	come
⑪	cut	cut	cut
⑫	do; does	did	done
⑬	draw	drew	drawn
⑭	drink	drank	drunk
⑮	drive	drove	driven
⑯	eat	ate	eaten
⑰	fall	fell	fallen
⑱	find	found	found
⑲	fly	flew	flown
⑳	forget	forgot	forgot; forgotten
㉑	get	got	got; gotten
㉒	give	gave	given
㉓	go	went	gone
㉔	grow	grew	grown
㉕	have; has	had	had
㉖	hear	heard	heard
㉗	keep	kept	kept
㉘	know	knew	known
㉙	leave	left	left

	simple present	simple past	past participle
㉚	lend	lent	lent
㉛	let	let	let
㉜	lose	lost	lost
㉝	make	made	made
㉞	meet	met	met
㉟	put	put	put
㊱	read	read	read
㊲	ride	rode	ridden
㊳	rise	rose	risen
㊴	run	ran	run
㊵	say	said	said
㊶	see	saw	seen
㊷	sell	sold	sold
㊸	send	sent	sent
㊹	shall	should	—
㊺	show	showed	shown; showed
㊻	sing	sang	sung
㊼	sit	sat	sat
㊽	sleep	slept	slept
㊾	speak	spoke	spoken
㊿	spend	spent	spent
(51)	stand	stood	stood
(52)	swim	swam	swum
(53)	take	took	taken
(54)	teach	taught	taught
(55)	tell	told	told
(56)	think	thought	thought
(57)	throw	threw	thrown
(58)	understand	understood	understood
(59)	will	would	—
(60)	write	wrote	written

Review 2 ▷ Oral Practice

Answer questions.

1. What do you usually eat for breakfast ?

2. When do you watch TV ?

3. Which day of the week is usually a busy day ?

4. How many people are there in your family ?

5. How much money do you have ?

6. Your father is a teacher, isn't he ?

7. Do you know the boy who is playing baseball in the park ?

8. What's your favorite activity ?

9. Are both you and your sister (brother) tall ? (neither ~ nor ~)

10. What have you decided to do tomorrow ?

11. Have you ever been to the U.S.A. before ?

12. **If you had a lot of money, what would you do ?**

13. **How long have you studied English ?**

14. **Can you speak English ?** (not only, but also)

15. **What does the food taste like?**

16. **How does your girlfriend** (boyfriend) **look ?**

17. **What makes you feel sad ?**

18. **What did you forget to do yesterday ?** (forget + to V.)

19. **Why is studying English important ?** (be spoken)

20. **What do you want to eat in the fast-food restaurant ?** (either ~ or ~)

21. **Can you hear the birds sing in the park ?**

(Note) : If your class can do this practice quite well, you can let them work in pairs and take turns asking and answering these questions.

Review 3 〉 Sing a Song

It's a Small World

1. It's a world of laugh-ter, a world of tears;
2. There is just one moon and one gold-en sun

it's a world of hopes and a world of fears.
and a smile means friend-ship to ev - 'ry one.

There's so much that we share that it's time we're a - ware.
Though the moun-tains di - vide and the o - ceans are wide,

It's a small world af - ter all. _____
It's a small world af - ter all. _____

Fine

It's a small world af - ter all, It's a

small world af - ter all. It's a small world

af - ter all, It's a small, small world. _____

D.C.

第 五 冊 學 習 內 容 一 覽 表

單元	內 容	練 習	活 動	習 作
複習第四冊	(1) A.我星期一來 B.你的生日是什麼時候？ (2) 誰最胖？ (3) 我昨天打網球 (4) 我將唸英文	Look and read. Look and say. Look and say. Look and say. Look and say.		
1	瑪麗是個好女孩 總是、通常和經常	Look and say：看圖練習各種頻率副詞，如 always, usually, often 等的用法。	韻律：Listen to Me.	Rearrange the sentences.
2	數 量 (一)	Read and match：利用連連看練習 some, a little, any, a few 等。	遊戲：What am I doing ?	Answer questions
3	數 量 (二)	Choose the correct one：利用選擇題複習 a lot of, many, much 及前面教過的數量形容詞。	歌曲：If you are happy.	Make sentences.
4	這是你的狗，不是嗎？	Answer questions：口說練習，造附加問句。	遊戲：Get the apple.	Make tag-questions.
5	被動態 動詞三態	Read and do：閱讀一段短文故事，將圖片重新組合。	歌曲：Looby Loo	Rearrange the sentences.
6	關係代名詞 who, which 和 that	Look and say：從圖片中練習將 2 個句子用關係代名詞連接起來。	遊戲：Make a guess.	Make sentences.
7	我喜歡烹飪	Look and read：列出動名詞當主詞及 like, love, hate, enjoy 等動詞的句型。	遊戲：Tongue twisters.	Look and write. Look and say. Look and write.
8	嚐起來很好吃	Look and say：練習 not only ～, but also ～ 及連綴動詞如 feel, sound, taste 等接形容詞的句型。	歌曲：Edelweiss	Answer questions
9	酸葡萄	Look and say：看圖練習 so ～ that 及 too ～ to 的句型。	歌曲：Sing	Change the sentences. Join the sentences.
10	多可怕！ 感官動詞和使役動詞	Look and say：看圖練習用 how 和 what 造感嘆句。	遊戲：Make a paper crane.	Make sentences.
11	either 和 neither 我也是	Look and say：看圖練習造 either ～or ～, 及 neither ～ nor ～ 的句型。	歌曲：Do-Re-Mi.	Look and write.
12	我已經讀過了 美國之旅	Look and say：2 人一組，看圖練習現在完成式的問答對話。 Say and write：告訴同伴你的寒假計劃。	遊戲：Who did what ?	Make sentences.
13	你會怎麼辦？	Look and say：看圖練習條件式的假設句及與現在事實相反的假設句。	歌曲：Donna Donna	Make sentences.
複習	(1) 不規則動詞三態表 (2) 口說練習 (3) 歌曲	Answer questions. It's a small world.		

國立教育資料館審核通過！

學習兒童美語讀本⑤

編　　著 / 陳怡平

發 行 所 / 學習出版有限公司　　　　☎ (02) 2704-5525

郵 撥 帳 號 / 05127272 學習出版社帳戶

登 記 證 / 局版台業 2179 號

印 刷 所 / 裕強彩色印刷有限公司

台 北 門 市 / 台北市許昌街 10 號 2 F　　☎ (02) 2331-4060

台灣總經銷 / 紅螞蟻圖書有限公司　　　☎ (02) 2795-3656

本公司網址　www.learnbook.com.tw

電 子 郵 件　learnbook@learnbook.com.tw

書 + MP3 一片售價：新台幣二百八十元正

2015 年 11 月 1 日新修訂

ISBN 978-986-231-107-3